CW00866561

THE MAGIC BLANKET FORT

KEITH KELLY

This book is dedicated to my Grandson Lucas.
I love you so much.

ACKNOWLEDGMENTS

I would like to thank Lucas Forcier for inspiring me to
write this book, Dana Darrow for
helping with the editing process, and all of my family and
friends for their undying support.

CHAPTER ONE

MID-MORNING ON SEPTEMBER 11, 2009, MY Grandson Charlie arrives into the world, weighing a healthy six-pound eight-ounces. Our faces are streaked with tears as they river themselves down our cheeks. My wife, my daughter and I are beside ourselves with contentment, peace, and joy to meet this wonderful gift of life. My wife and I stand around my daughter's bedside, looking down at her. My wife's hands caressing my daughter's forehead as she holds this bundle of joy close to her chest, smiling proudly, knowing she is a mother. My offspring had a rough go of it, being on bed rest the last couple of months of her pregnancy. All of us experience relief when Charlie is born. My name is Ben and from the instant holding this little breathing life in my arms, he becomes my best friend.

People say they witness love at first sight; that's true because I am in love the minute I see this little guy. Charlie is a good baby, eating and sleeping well, and never crying at night. Sue, my wife, and I keep him as much as possible as we love him being around. He spends the night often.

As Charlie grows, he smiles, frowns, and laughs when he hears familiar voices. He observes everything. The moment we turn on the television or music, that little boy looks towards it and smiles. He loves music. When the radio plays, he hums to the music with his baby sounds. Charlie tries his best to sing.

I have forgotten how hard and tiring it can be taking care of a little one. Just as we relax on the couch, he cries, and one of us has to get up and go check on this baby. Usually, we both get up and creep down the hall to spy in to see what he is doing. Many times, he is looking at the ceiling kicking his little legs all around, his blanket thrown to the corner of his crib.

———

TIME ZOOMS BY, and Charlie can sit up on his own. Sue and I take so many pictures as we are proud of him. Even at this young age, he likes to come to Grandma and Grandpa's to spend time with us.

Soon enough, he crawls, getting into everything. This is when I have to childproof the house by covering the plugs and such. Perhaps a little overprotective as our place is like Fort Knox secured from any harm to our little grandbaby. Since the moment he crawls, showing autonomy, he doesn't like anyone holding him and will squirm his way loose, and off he crawls. I figure his character will be that of independence, freethinking, and curiosity.

Charlie begins walking at an average age for children and moves quickly. The wife and I take him out in the backyard, and he takes off, running as fast as his little feet will carry him. Believe me, it feels exhausting chasing after him, making sure he doesn't trip and hurt himself. Charlie spends the night with us every Tuesday as Geri, my daughter, works the night shift. By the time Charlie falls asleep on Tuesday nights, my wife and I are ready for bed as well.

Charlie is a late talker. He knows what various objects are but doesn't voice what they are. When he wants his sippy cup or a toy, he points to it and grunts. Even though he doesn't talk much, he has a keen sense of observation. He notices everything from a new picture on the wall to flowers his grandmother just placed on the table.

When he finally does start speaking, his first word is Mom, which brings my daughter to tears. Shortly after, he peers at my spouse and says, "Grandma." A week or so later, bouncing him on the bed, he looks at me and says, "Pah Pah," then I cry. Kids always come up with their own names to call their grandparents.

One evening, Charlie and I are rolling a ball back and forth on a blanket spread out on our front yard's grass. Charlie laughs and giggles as he swats at the ball, doing his best to roll the ball back to me. Sue and Geri sit nearby talking when Charlie points towards the city, which is visible from our front yard and says, "Albuquerque." He says this word so clear; it is impressive that such a complicated name is his fourth word.

"Did you hear that?" I ask them. They stop their chatter and listen.

We ask him to repeat it, and he does. After this, the kid talks non-stop.

Being a writer and telling him stories, it isn't long before Charlie becomes a storyteller. The names this kid makes up in his head, such as Sneener, PoPo, and Meno, are fantastic. Another character of his creation is Goo Goo Ga Gus. When I ask about these characters, he says they are his friends. He insists that Sneener and Goo Goo Ga Gus are boyfriend and girlfriend. I enjoy playing along with these tales and made-up characters.

Charlie has such a vivid imagination and God's given the benefit of creativity to this boy. At first, his stories consist of general things that boys make up in their imagination. However, around six years of age, his stories become very exact, more specific than what matches his age. Charlie describes scenes and characters beyond his age group's imagination. I ask where he gets these ideas, and he says they are real. I play along. What am I going to do? Tell a six-year-old little boy I don't believe his fables. Charlie has a blessed gift. I will never discourage it by suggesting I don't believe him.

CHAPTER TWO

TUESDAYS ARE MY FAVORITE DAY OF THE WEEK because Charlie spends the night. I see him almost every day, but Tuesday nights are the best because he stays over. Charlie loves water, water hoses, PVC pipes, washing machines, and vacuum cleaners. He is not your typical kid. Most kids his age love toys such as cars and trains; he prefers constructing things with pipes or hoses.

He and I connect them across the backyard and throughout the house. He enjoys connecting pipes into a sturdy frame and then spreading a sheet over them, making a fort. Every week we build a blanket fort and fall asleep in it until morning. This is our special thing to do, and I hope that Charlie will remember these times spent together.

On Tuesday after dinner, Charlie and I go to the hardware store to purchase some roofing repair materials. As we walk by the PVC, I hope Charlie doesn't see the pipes because if he does, he will want me to buy some for that night's blanket fort. Sure enough, Charlie notices the pipes and talks me into buying new ones, six-foot ones. This means when arriving home, I will have to cut them into sections and smooth the ends down so that the size will be right to build the fort in Charlie's bedroom.

Once home, I put the roofing materials away, stacking them neatly in the corner. I set up my sawhorses, get my little saw, and begin the cutting. Charlie sits on the garage floor and watches, handing me another pipe when I am ready. I cut the pipes into smaller pieces, examine the ends for rough edges, and give them to Charlie. He sands the ends smooth with sandpaper and then stacks them neatly in the middle of the garage. I watch him as he organizes them and finds it amazing that he takes the time to do that. Excited, my grandson helps me carry them into his bedroom, and we build the best blanket fort ever. Blankets lie over the structure of PVC pipes as if sleeping.

Within fifteen minutes, together, we have constructed the evening's fort. This fort is our best one yet, sturdier than expected, and the blankets take the shape of the frame well. Scotch tape and shoestrings secure the blankets to the PVC frame and bedposts. Bedtime rolls around, so the two of us situate ourselves under the blankets, and I read him a story, and we laugh and tell jokes. I love to hear Charlie laugh, and he loves to listen to me laugh. I am the happiest man alive to have this little youngster in my life. We are the best of friends. Together we've built many forts, but this one is different. Charlie says these pipes are magic, and he is correct.

As I mentioned, Charlie has always been a great storyteller with a keen imagination; he insists his adventures are real, and I play along. But, one Tuesday night all of that changed. What I am about to say to you is true. I was there.

"Pah Pah, this fort is magic."

"Oh yeah, how so, grandson?"

"Let's go to sleep and you will see when you wake up Pah Pah."

"Ok, Charlie, I love you."

"Love you too, Pah Pah."

———

THE SLIGHTEST OF breezes wake me at sunrise, which is strange because I can't figure where the breeze is coming from. I know I didn't leave a window open, so I throw off the covers stepping out of the fort to the most peaceful sunrise.

"What the heck, where are we? Wake up, Charlie."

Charlie rises, rubbing his eyes, sits up, and says, "I told you this fort was magic Pah Pah."

"Do you know where we are, Charlie?"

"I don't know, but not at your house, let's go."

Charlie sprints off, running full speed across what is the most delightful green meadow I ever encounter. Both of us feel peace and safety; I wish everyone could feel it. How did Charlie know this? Somehow, we wake up in this strange land that Charlie can't wait to explore. Chasing after him, urging him to stop and wait for me, he just keeps running. We stop at a river where the most beautiful blue water flows. The taste is sweet as I swallow. Behind us, a carved-out tree trunk full of drink and fruits.

"What is this place, Charlie?"

"Magic, Pah Pah, it's magic."

"Good day fellows," a voice sounds.

Startled, we turn to see a strange-looking being. This fellow, or thing, or something, resembles tumbleweeds blowing in the summer winds back home in New Mexico except for being pink with green stripes around it. It bounces like a ball over to us, introducing himself as Sneener. Sneener holds out a bristly arm, shaking our hands, welcoming us.

"What is this place?" I ask.

"The earth of Torrox, we've been expecting you, and receive you with open arms."

Hundreds of pink creatures emerge from the woods, chanting a welcome chant.

"What are they saying, Charlie?"

"They are saying welcome from King PoPo."

"Why do you understand them, and I don't?"

"Because I am a kid, Pah Pah."

Sneener leads us to a castle to meet King PoPo. The castle is plain, but its peacefulness makes it beautiful. Never have I felt such calmness. My limbs are relaxed and limp. Charlie's excited and giddy, happier than usual. Once before King PoPo, we take a seat at a massive table of food. King PoPo says the kingdom has been expecting us.

"Why are we here?" I ask.

"To have fun, Pah Pah."

"I'm asking King PoPo."

"You are here for a reason which will reveal itself in time. Just know we want to share our land with you because we feel you and your grandson have goodness in your hearts."

"How do we get back home?"

"Just ask, but stay a while and enjoy? You can return home anytime you wish, and no time will have passed, it's as if you never left."

Charlie begs to stay for a while. I give in, so that's what we do. That night we sleep in a lovely room overlooking a brook, flowing with harmonious sounds of birds and violins and wind blowing through tree branches in harmony. The land is beautiful, but it will take a while to get used to the strange creatures. These creatures refer to themselves as beings. The males pink with green stripes and the females green with pink stripes. They have bristly arms, and their appearance reminds me of a spray-painted tumbleweed. Whenever they want to move short distances they hop around. To move long distances, they tuck their arms in and the breeze rolls them like a ball. When the wind is blowing hard, they stay indoors because it blows them away out of their control.

Sneener says there are other beings in the area that are part being and part human, known as the blue people but, are seldom spotted. Charlie likes Sneener. He thinks the beings are funny and fun to play with. The Ga Ga Galugas Tribe inhabits this village of Ga Ga

Galugas. Kings name all cities in the land of Torrox after the tribes that settled them. They've existed several thousand years, sending for human visitors every so often. Kings only allow humans of goodness as visitors to the land.

"What do you think, grandson, want to stay awhile?"

"Yes, Pah Pah,"

"Cool, we will see what we find in this adventure."

The first week is impressive.

Charlie and I receive celebrity treatment. The local tribe members bring food for us every day, making us feel at home. Charlie and I explore the countryside and enjoy the landscape. I have no clue what this place is, but it's nothing like I've ever seen. Both of us like it, and as long as time stands still back home, we plan on staying a while. Sneener and Charlie have become good friends, playing together every day.

It is coming up on Spector, which is a rainy season in Torrox. Spector lasts for three weeks, and beings usually stay in their homes across the land. Everyone is making and storing food, preparing for these three weeks.

Not sure how Charlie will do cooped up in a castle for three weeks, I prepare myself. I'm not sure how I will do either. I ask Charlie if he wants to return home, but he begs to stay. King PoPo mentions we would be fine in the rains, but as far as the beings, the water weighs them down, and they can't move well, so most stay indoors. King PoPo says the rainbows will appear and that Charlie and I should travel to them and visit the mean old lady.

"If she is mean, why would we visit her?" I ask.

"She isn't that mean, she is just a grouchy old lady who tries to set her nahs on visitors."

"Nahs?" I ask.

"That's like dogs in your land, except nahs hop on one leg and shaped like what humans would call a football. Their skin is even brown and leathery like one. The mean old lady lives at the end of the rainbow. Cantankerous old bat, yes, but she is harmless."

We are up for that, so within the next couple of days, the rainbows appear, and we are off. As we stroll across the meadow, the rain subsides, and the weather is neither hot nor too cold. We talk about our journey and the magic blanket fort. Charlie says he can't wait to tell his friends and his teacher Mrs. Plant. I think of being a child and how Charlie can share this experience. If I discuss this, people will conclude I am a looney.

"I want you to understand, Charlie, that whenever you're ready to go home, we can."

"Ok Pah Pah, but I am having fun,"

"I just want you to know we can return whenever we want."

By mid-morning, we reach the rainbow. The colors are vivid, illuminating the most beautiful blues, pink, and orange I have ever seen. We take our backpacks off, sitting them on the ground, standing and looking in awe for several minutes. We climb up and slide down the side for hours laughing and having fun. One side of the rainbow is short, the other long. It is a short climb and a long slide, just perfect. After spending two hours sliding down the rainbow, Charlie and I enjoy lying on our backs on the soft ground looking up through a cover of heavy trees as the sun struggles to bathe us with its rays. Only for brief moments, the sun peers through the thickness of the wood branches. It is perfect. The tree limbs clothed in leaves shield the sun just enough not to blind us. The tree branches cut the sun in sections creating rays that burst forth over the woods' roof. Noticing the rays of the sunlight, I wonder how far they can reach. Just because I can't see their light anymore, does that mean they stop? The wood's so thick it's like a room safe from the outside world.

We spy two birds, and I am sure they notice us and probably wonder what we are doing in their room. I wonder what they are thinking of Charlie and me being there. Who knows, maybe they like us here, or perhaps they don't even notice. They are chirping wildly, so I make up a conversation between them.

"Charlie, I can speak bird, you know."

"Yea, right, Pah Pah."

"I can. You want to know what they are talking about?"

"Sure."

"Well, I'll tell you. Here goes."

"Who are those humans down there?" the first bird asks.

"I don't know," the second bird answers. "Should we check things out?"

"Not yet, let's see what they do."

"Humans are different," the second bird says.

"How so?"

"Well, they come to the woods for fun, just to look around, while we're here to hunt and reproduce. Strange, huh?" the second bird asks.

"Probably so."

Both Charlie and I laugh as I dream up their conversation. I suppose they are communicating in their way; all creatures do. Nature is something I love. I tell Charlie I'd rather be outside than inside unless it is raining or snowing. When I was a boy, I'd like to look up at the clouds for what seemed like forever, seeing shapes of animals and people.

The warmth of the sun finds us under the thick canvas of overgrown trees giving me peace and reminds me of looking at the clouds when I was a kid. This makes me feel thankful to have Charlie to share this adventure with.

The forest voice of birds chirping, the wind rustling the leaves, and the water flowing to a rhythm in the brook, I find peaceful and relaxing. Charlie and I close our eyes and listen to the sounds that surround us. We lay beside each other, holding hands in such peace. I hear Charlie breathe the breath of life and think about how wonderful he is.

"Do animals know what life is? Do they know they are alive?" Charlie asks.

"I always wonder that myself," I tell him.

I explain to him that nature is so important and that it is a connection to our spirit.

We love this forest room, the little birds above talking, and all the sounds of this beautiful life.

CHAPTER THREE

THE RAINS BEGIN AGAIN, SO WE CONTINUE TO THE mean old lady's house. King PoPo sends a cake with us to give to Deeky. A quarter of a mile past the end of the rainbow, in a clearing, stands the mean old lady's cabin, just as King PoPo describes. Two nahs come bouncing towards us. We stand still. The nahs lick Charlie, almost knocking the boy down. King PoPo is right; nahs are not mean at all. As we approach the cabin, walking side by side, I am looking all around us cautiously. Charlie is too distracted by the nahs to notice his surroundings. The mean old lady staggers to the porch, hollering at us, asking who we are, and ordering us to leave. The porch is grey and rickety, almost ready to collapse. This differed from what I expected. Her rich green color and bristles thick like the younger beings we met in the village. Older one's color fades, and their bristles thin. Deeky, however, displays vibrancy. She rolls clumsily, and as King PoPo says, "Grouchy."

"King PoPo sent you this cake," I say.

"Leave it to brother to send gifts with strangers."

"Bored with the rainy season, we thought we'd leave on an adventure and come visit you."

The mean old lady laughed, saying, "PoPo sent you here to check up on me, he worries about me too much."

"I didn't realize he was your brother, ma'am."

"Don't call me ma'am! I don't want you to come inside, but since it's raining and you two are here, you may. I love children, they are always welcome, it's adults I don't like."

"Your brother is right, you like to grouch," I say.

"What's your name, little.... humans call you a boy, right?" Deeky asks.

"Yes, ma'am," Charlie says.

"You are the cutest thing I have seen since brother was a small being."

Thanks, mean old lady."

"Call me Deeky."

"That's an interesting name," I comment.

"It's my father's name."

Charlie bonds with Deeky. Deeky invites us to stay as long as we wish.

Over the next several days, we play games, and she teaches Charlie how to bake cookies, and she becomes like a second grandmother. I work around her cabin, helping with chores. Deeky comes to admire us and appreciates my help. After dinner in the evenings, we sit out on her porch, and Deeky shares stories of her childhood and of the land, such as how all of the kings and villages came to existence. She also tells us about how her parents passed in a rockslide and afterward it was just her and PoPo. She raised and protected him. Charlie also tells her a story or about himself.

Charlie loves looking for treasure and tells us that he found a quarter last week searching for treasure in his backyard. This creates excitement and gives him the idea to gather his friends and go on a treasure hunt through the neighborhood. That afternoon he and his friends make a list of random things and walk around the neighborhood, ringing doorbells, asking for them. The first one to collect everything on the list wins the treasure hunt.

This is right up Charlie's alley, he loves searching for treasure, and he thinks this will be the most fantastic fun ever. Their list consisted of a yellow shoestring, a red piece of construction paper, two paperclips, an old dishrag, two pencils (used), an empty bottle, and a Snickers bar. The gang figures they will get hungry.

The first house Charlie approaches is the Brooks' house. Mrs. Brooks gives him two paper clips. After that, he arrives at the Smith house, where Mr. Smith gives him a Snickers bar.

He hit the jackpot. Charlie pretends to be a good pirate searching for gold. Charlie attains all the items except for the pencils, so he sits on the curb to eat his Snickers bar. Chocolate melts on his fingers as he licks it off, finding that's the best part. He balls up the wrapper stuffing it in his jeans pocket to prove to his friends he got it in the treasure hunt. Charlie chooses a shortcut back towards his house. As he walks, he kicks rocks loose from the dirt, finding a ten-dollar bill. Feeling so excited, he almost loses his breath. This treasure isn't on the list. The boys all meet at the end of the street, forming a circle to show each other their treasures. Charlie digs deep down in his front pocket, first pulling out the candy bar wrapper and then the best prize of all, the ten-dollar bill. He unfolds it, straightens it out, grasping it on each end, and snaps it in mid-air, getting their attention.

He wants to share this treasure with his friends, so one of the boy's mothers drives Charlie and his friends to Ashburn's Ice Cream Parlor, and they have a soda, cake, and ice cream.

He has money left over to buy himself two packs of bubble gum. After finding the money, they forget about finishing the treasure hunt game. Still, Charlie has more items than his friends, so he figures he is the winner.

The next day Charlie takes the shortcut as he kicks rocks looking for more money with no luck but feels fortunate to have found the money and taken his friends for a good day of eating sweets.

"I didn't know that, Charlie."

"Yeah, Pah Pah, I forgot to tell you about it."

"Well, that shows character that you share with others, and it is a special gift looking for treasures," Deeky responds.

Deeky asks questions about our land and what it is like. I tell her that her land looks like a fantasy land. She can't understand why someone would think her land is a fantasy land. It's just a place for her.

Deeky and Charlie grow attached. Charlie doesn't want to leave Deeky's hut, so we stay a while.

We had been at Deeky's a month when Sneener shows up. The King sends him to check up on us since we have been away from the kingdom longer than expected. Sneener is relieved to see we'd all taken to each other. Deeky shares the story of taking Sneener many years ago when he wandered up to her place one evening. He took away from his village because he didn't like how his village treated other towns, nor how the king treated them. His village was the Grangus tribe. Most of the twenty tribes dislike them in this land. He wanted to get away and start over. He came across Deeky's cabin, and she took him in for several years. She introduced him to her twin, King PoPo, and that's when he moved to and joined the Ga Ga Galugas tribe.

It's nice to have Sneener around, and Charlie enjoys playing chase and tag with him. Sneener plans to stay for a week and then return to Ga Ga Galugas.

Even though Charlie and I enjoy ourselves in this new land, at night I check with Charlie to see if he is ready to go home. Charlie always says no because he is enjoying the company of Deeky.

She enjoys having someone to cook for, and we show appreciation. It feels good to make her happy. Deeky makes the best-fried rabbit I have eaten since being a boy living in the country.

Deeky is a grumpy sort but not as bad as her reputation. One evening after dinner, I ask her why she has this reputation. She says it started many years ago when raising her brother, King PoPo. Deeky was the only mother figure he had, and she was strict with him. One day he was out hunting and got home way after dark, and she had worried herself sick. Near bedtime, PoPo and his friend Meeno finally came home. *They drank too many* fermented berries losing track of time. Deeky tore into them with the wrath of a demon, making them cry. Meeno peed himself as he felt the fear rise in his body. Deeky woke them for two months solid at dawn, making them do chores. Meeno began calling her mean old lady. Being his name was Meeno, and to him, she seemed like an old lady. Instead of people saying Meno called her a mean old lady, it changed to Meno lady to shorten the phrase and story.

The story spread around the countryside of how she was a mean old witch. At least for a hundred years, people stayed away from her because of the tale she stole children. Still, the King's men caught the real witch over in a nearby village, so everyone realized it wasn't her.

"Tell us the tale, Deeky," Charlie asks.

"I guess I can."

There once was a creepy witch named Deeky.
With hair white as snow.
She would steal children in the night.
When the sun lifted, she'd let them go.

The children would go home and tell,
but parents didn't believe,
until one day

they listened to a little boy named Pareve.

During the night when the witch stole the
    children
they screamed for their parents.
The parents rushed to their room but
all that was there, a broom.

They called the King's men
begging for help, but
nothing could be done
for anyone.

Until the sun rose
and the children
returned home.
Lights in their room are shown.

She got caught in the light
by the King's men
never to steal
another child at night.

She went to jail.

"Is that true, Deeky?" Charlie asks.
"Yes, but her real name was Esmeralda, and she had a
habit of stealing folks' nahs and goats, not their kids.
After the kids got mad at me, they spread it around, but it
didn't last long."

CHAPTER FOUR

THREE WEEKS PASS WHEN ONE EVENING AT DUSK, A courier from King PoPo's castle comes to Deeky's. We all sit down at a tree stump as Deeky serves us rabbit and water for dinner. Slatch, the messenger, reports he is there to check up on Sneener as he is due back at the village. I explain that Sneener left three weeks ago to return to the castle. Slatch informs us he has not arrived. Slatch is concerned that perhaps Sneener's born tribe, the Grangus, may have kidnapped him and taken him back to their village.

"We have to go find him, Pah Pah,"

"Yes, we do, Charlie, but it is the tribe's work," Slatch responds.

"He came here to check on us, we want to help," I say.

"Good enough then, we will leave at sunup."

That night as Charlie and I lay in our pallet, Charlie says,

"Pah Pah, will we find my friend Sneener?"

"I hope so, grandson, we sure will try."

"We will try?"

"We will, grandson."

————

THE NEXT MORNING the sun began peeking over the ridge; it brought yet another messenger from King PoPo with news that Slatch's bride has taken ill, and he has to return to Ga Ga Galugas. This concerns me because I was counting on Slatch leading the path to search for Sneener. I share my thoughts with Slatch as we sit at the morning fire nibbling on rabbit. I want to talk with him before Charlie wakes.

"Not to worry," Slatch says. "Take this crystal ball and it will show you the way through the country to Grangus."

In a short time, Slatch packs a handkerchief of rabbit in his bag, and we all say goodbye.Slatch tucks his arms and legs in close to his bristly body, looking like a tumble-weed, and the wind blows him towards his home. Slatch hurries back to King PoPo's castle while Charlie and I take the crystal ball and begin our journey to find Sneener. Charlie finds this land beautiful, much different from back home. Charlie knew the blanket fort to be magic when we built it. I don't understand how, but we are having fun on this journey. As we walk, we come upon the most beautiful spectacle—a flowing river of chocolate.

"Pah Pah look! look!"

"Now that's a sight to see."

Pieces of cotton candy floating on streams of soda pop. We hop on one, and away we float down the stream.

"*What is this place?*" Charlie asks. "This is the most fascinating place ever. Rivers of soda pop, and floating on cotton candy with you, Pah Pah, what could be better than this?"

As the river becomes shallow and we no longer can float, we jump from the candy pieces and walk along the bank. The moon's on the rise, so we stop for the night and set up our tent. Charlie and I lay in the tent looking into the crystal ball, studying our way to Grangus. The crystal ball reveals that we have to follow the yellow star shining in the daytime sky. The crystal ball shows a swamp to cross, which concerns me about how we will go about crossing it. Slatch said the crystal ball will show us the path. I believe that and reassure Charlie that as long as we have the crystal ball, we won't get lost.

The morning comes, and the sun rises bright and beautiful. I pull out boiled eggs from my pack that Deeky made for us.

"Pah Pah, I want strawberry milk."

That's Charlie's favorite drink back home.

"We don't have strawberry milk, baby, sorry."

Suddenly besides the crystal ball, a glass of warm strawberry milk appears.

"Did you do that, Pah Pah?"

"No, the crystal ball did it."

"The crystal ball, Pah Pah?"

"Yes, it seems so."

Charlie expresses happiness; we eat, drink, pack up the tent, and head along the river to Grangus. I am leading the way as Charlie walks behind me looking at all of his surroundings. Charlie carries the crystal ball admiring its beauty, when suddenly, out of the sky, a giant creature with two heads and wings swoops down and swipes it away from him. This bird-like creature flies off. It's a peculiar-looking thing, twice as big as me with six legs that look like switch sticks. Purple with the most horrific screech I ever heard. We need that ball. Slatch said it's what will get us to the village where Sneener may be.

We have to search for the purple bird to obtain the crystal ball before searching for Sneener. Without it, we can't find a way to him.

"Charlie, perhaps we should travel back to Deeky's, we don't even know if Sneener is in his old village."

"He is, Pah Pah."

"How do you know grandson?"

"Same as I knew our blanket fort was magic."

The purple creature flies above us in circles, taunting us or perhaps wanting us to follow. Therefore, that's what we do. When we rest, the bird lands several feet away from us, guarding the crystal ball.

"What do you think he wants, Pah Pah?"

"To follow him," I say.

We follow it for hours until reaching the huge swamp the crystal ball revealed the evening before. The black swamp stretches as far as my sight. There's no way of getting around it or swimming through it. If only that bird hadn't taken our crystal ball, we could wish for a boat. Just as we turn around and begin heading back to Deeky's, the purple creature lands on the black water spreading his wings.

"He wants us to get on his back, Pah Pah, like I do yours when we play piggyback rides."

"Maybe your right, grandson."

So, we climb on the bird's back, and he uses his six feet as paddles and carries us to the other side of the black swamp. On the other side, the enormous purple bird gives the crystal ball back to Charlie and flies towards the sun.

"Well, Pah Pah, Slatch said the crystal ball would show us the way, I guess it did."

"Yep, it did."

We continue our journey. The crystal ball serves as our guide through the swamp and to Grangus. Charlie blames himself for Sneener getting kidnapped or lost because he came to check on us.

As we make our way through the beautiful country-side, we talk and laugh.

"Knock knock," Charlie replies.

"Who's there?"

"Knock knock," Charlie says again.

"Who's there?"

"Knock knock."

"Charlie, why do you keep saying that?"

"That's the joke, Pah Pah."

Charlie doesn't understand what knock-knock jokes are, so he thinks that that's the real joke. I explain, and we laugh so hard I have to sit down on the ground. We decide to nap for a while as Charlie lies crossways using my stomach as his pillow. I mainly lie with my legs crossed, looking up at the sky, noticing it's different from the sky back home. The sky here is a light purple instead of blue, and the clouds are red. At that moment, we hear a noise from the bushes alongside the trail. To our surprise, the strangest-looking being we've seen thus far strides from the brush alongside us.

"What's your business here?" the being asks.

"Pah Pah, he can talk."

"We are seeking a lost friend," I answer.

This being is blue, standing only a few inches from the ground with long front legs and short back legs as if he is pointing to the sky. The creature resembles a praying mantis, but blue and as big as a basset hound, poised close to the ground with a long tubular body.

"What's your lost friend's name?"

"Sneener," Charlie answers.

"Hmm... how'd he get lost?"

"My grandson and I believe his old tribe kidnapped him."

"Why would they kidnap your friend?"

"He used to be in their tribe, and he left to be in the Ga Ga Galugas tribe," I explain.

"Oh, I see," he says.

The creature introduces himself as Bill and says most of his family appears gold with pink eyes and black feet, but he turned out to be blue. Because of this, the villagers refer to him as Blue Bill.

"Pah Pah, Sneener and King PoPo mentioned the blue people, remember?"

"Yes, I do."

Blue Bill joins the search and is a good tracker. I reveal we have the crystal ball to instruct us. Blue Bill informs us the crystal ball is outdated and will not guide during a thunderstorm. Blue Bill insists on traveling with us. I will keep an eye on this being.

As the three of us travel closer to Grangus, walking side by side through grass and rocks, the weather is perfect. I mention the magic blanket fort, how Charlie and I fell asleep waking to find ourselves in this world.

"Time stands still while you're here. You can look into the crystal ball and see you and Charlie sleeping in your blanket fort in your world," Bill says.

We look into it, and sure enough, we are sleeping. The clock reads 10 p.m., which is the time we went to bed.

Up ahead in the distance, we view a green mountain. The rocks shape themselves as though the ridge wears a smile. Blue Bill tells us it's the mountain of joy.

"Can we go there, Pah Pah?"

"I suppose we can. Is that ok, Blue Bill?"

"Humans visit once every few years so they will let you visit. The beings will treat both of you like kings."

"Hip hip hooray," Charlie says anxiously.

"The mountain is further than it looks, little boy. It will take two hours. We should stop at the brook up ahead for a drink."

We reach the brook and sit down on a broken tree and talk.

"Maybe Joy Mountain is your purpose for being here," Blue Bill says.

"Purpose?" Charlie replies.

"Yes. Humans always come here for a purpose; it will reveal itself in time,"

Blue Bill continues to say the last humans that visited were brother and sister.

"No one's sure why it happens?" Blue Bill replies. "I wonder why we crossed paths today. There is a reason for sure."

An hour later, the three of us reach Joy Mountain and are greeted by the strange-looking beings as the three of us walk single file down a dusty road towards their village.

Blue Bill was right. They are people of joy. Their heads resemble humans but with bigger eyes, and their bodies invisible. All you see is their heads floating around mid-air. This scares Charlie a little at first, but he is ok when he realizes how friendly these beings are. We all sit down at a flat rock table for a feast, as if the inhabitants knew we were coming. Gathered around the table, there were at least a hundred beings. They were laughing and very friendly towards us. They asked questions of our land, and we asked questions of theirs. They served us first before they began eating. I shared our pursuit of a friend.

One inhabitant said a stranger passed through last

week named Sneener headed for Grangus to find his love Goo Goo Ga Gus.

"We must continue our search first thing in the dawn," Blue Bill says.

I wonder why Blue Bill is so interested in finding Sneener, but I don't ask. Blue Bill acts rushed and seems anxious for the morning as if he wants to see Sneener for some reason as well. I keep a close eye on Blue Bill. That evening we turn in early, and in the middle of the night, Charlie wakes from a sound sleep thrashing anxiously and throwing his covers, looking under them and then all around him, realizing he doesn't have the crystal ball. He sleeps with it every night. He looks over to where Blue Bill is bunked down and sees he is gone.

"Pah Pah, wake up."

"What's wrong, Charlie?"

"The crystal ball and Blue Bill are gone."

"What!"

I look around, stand quickly putting on my boots, then walk over to where Bill slept. Sure enough, both are gone. Something is fishy about the way Blue Bill is acting. What I can't figure is why Blue Bill took the crystal ball. He already knows the way to Grangus.

"Fishy,"

"What does that mean, Pah Pah?"

"It means he is acting weird,"

Joy Mountain's inhabitants reveal to me over a conversation at breakfast that Blue Bill is a troublemaker, and they were hesitant to let him stay the night. The other beings act nervous and start gathering their things, offering to help us find Blue Bill because they feel he is up to something. Talking over food and drink at the rock table, King Lor of Green Mountain says, "Hmmm...Blue Bill wants to get to Sneener before you and your grandson do. Why, I wonder?"

"I don't know King Lor, but I had a feeling last night after he acted rushed to leave at first light that he may be up to something."

One of the inhabitants gives us a fast logi to ride, which is similar to a horse, to catch up with Blue Bill. The inhabitant tells us that the logi is an excellent tracker.

"Good, because Blue Bill has the crystal ball," Charlie tells the being.

In a flash, we're off to catch Blue Bill and reach Sneener first. Two of the Green Mountain beings accompany us. The weather turns cold, rainy, but steadily we ride through. The two beings are in the lead, then myself and Charlie following closely behind. We stop often to rest and to wrap up in our tarps to stay dry. We find a dry place under a rock outcropping when we need it most. Sitting no more than five minutes, Charlie feels something crawl over his leg and hears a squeaky voice say,

"What's the big idea, you're smothering me, you sat on me."

Charlie looks down and sees a purple snake slithering over the thigh of his leg to get by the fire for warmth.

Charlie jumps to his feet quickly and runs about three feet away from the snake. As Charlie slips and falls in the mud, he yells, "Pah Pah. There is a talking snake."

The snake tells Charlie not to be frightened and that he is a friend.

"I'm Snakey, what's your name?"

Charlie feels more comfortable as he slowly stands up covered in mud from his waist down.

"I am Charlie, and this is my Pah Pah."

"What are you two doing out in weather like this?"

"Looking for our friend Sneener."

"Popular friend. Blue Bill is searching for him."

"Did you see Blue Bill?" I ask.

"He passed by here this morning."

"We have to find him before Blue Bill does."

"Blue Bill has had it out for Sneener for years."

"Blue Bill knows Sneener?" I ask.

"Yes."

"Blue Bill confesses feelings on Goo Goo Ga Gus," Sankey replies.

"I thought Goo Goo Ga Gus is Sneener's girlfriend."

"There's the problem. It still upsets Blue Bill because she dumped him for Sneener."

"That's why Blue Bill is so interested in helping us find Sneener. He is looking for him himself."

"Will Blue Bill hurt Sneener?" Charlie asks.

"I am not sure, but we have to find Sneener before Blue Bill does."

Snakey predicts that Blue Bill is camping over the ridge, about an hour away in the only clearing for miles. We keep moving, even though it's raining. Snakey urges us to wait the storm out, but we want to get to Grangus first. There is no telling what Blue Bill may do to reclaim his beloved Goo Goo Ga Gus.

"So how far does this feud go back?"

Two hundred years. Blue Bill and Sneener used to be best friends until Goo Goo Ga Gus came into their lives.

"It was not a good time."

Snakey says they were five hundred years old when it all happened. They were going to naughen, which is a class taught by the Kings of each tribe. In this class, they teach students to be mediators to settle disagreements between tribes. Anyway, all three of them were in class one day when the King's assistant walked into the teaching room, introducing her to the class.

She is the first female in the class and the most beautiful being they have ever seen. She has long, lovely thick bristles that drag the ground in perfect sequence, swishing back and forth like they have a life of their own —all held in place by pink twine. Sneener is holding several writing sticks, and when he sees Goo Goo Ga Gus, he drops them all over the floor. He quickly reaches down to pick them up, his eyes never leaving Goo Goo Ga Gus.

"Class this is Goo Goo Ga Gus, she is from Grangus and is the first female student."

Snakey said when they were all growing up that Sneener was shy, but Blue Bill was outgoing and loud. So, on that first day when they met Goo Goo Ga Gus, Blue Bill asked her to sit with him to eat. Both boys sat admiring her the rest of the afternoon instead of the slate rock where the teacher was writing the day's lessons.

Near the end of the day, Sneener builds up enough nerve to sit by her and begin a conversation.

"My name is Sneener, I would like to show you around the village and be your acquaintance."

"I would like that divinely, Sneener."

They roll away together as the wind blows them slightly towards the village.

Blue Bill grows jealous. Sneener asks if he can walk her home after class. She smiles, exposing her beautiful gray teeth, and says,

"I'd like that."

After that, Sneener and Goo Goo Ga Gus have lunch together, talk, and laugh every day, while Blue Bill remains furious. He views the situation as Sneener stealing his girlfriend.

Blue Bill challenges Sneener to a duel. As Snakey tells Charlie and me the story, he drifts off to sleep, leaving us hanging. We never did find out what was the result of the duel.

CHAPTER FIVE

Meanwhile, during our journey to find Sneener, we wonder if Goo Goo Ga Gus realizes that Sneener is looking for her. According to Snakey, one hundred years have passed since she had seen him. Unknown to her and us at the time, Sneener is in captivity under the reign of King RiRa of Grangus; although it is one of the strictest tribes and sometimes not well-liked in the land, it is Goo Goo Ga Gus's home. Goo Goo Ga Gus and Sneener were planning to marry for two years when Sneener asked her to leave with him to join Ga Ga Galugas. She didn't prefer to go, and when King RiRa found out Sneener's plan to join another tribe, he prohibits him from Grangus, and if he comes back, the King will arrest him.

She is not aware he has returned and is in captivity in the village.

Goo Goo Ga Gus often thinks about Sneener and the fun they used to have. When he left the village, she missed him and sometimes still does. They were in love and spent every day together, laughing and playing under the stars.

Many nights she relaxes in her living room, looking at the sunset daydreaming of him.

She knows where he lives but doesn't possess the nerve to make the trip to see him. If she did and King RiRa found out, she would be banned from her home and the village. Goo Goo Ga Gus often reminisces about the week they spent camping by the river on Joy Mountain.

They were young and carefree and had nothing holding them back from being together and sharing a wonderful life together. This is when Snakey met them. As they camped by the river, Snakey slithered out to make their acquaintance. Sneener fed him and gave him a warm blanket to sleep under by the fire. They all sat up talking most of the night. Snakey was over five hundred years old, the oldest living thing Sneener or Goo Goo Ga Gus had met. They had heard of Snakey, but never thought he actually existed until then. Sneener knew there were not many snakes left in the land, so seeing and meeting him was a treat.

The villagers of Grangus and their parents always concluded they would end up being together, and they knew it too. It was an unsaid assumption, so when they broke up, the word traveled fast, perhaps the most important news that had hit their small village in years. This had already been a hundred years ago.

Snakey saw a vision of all this away back then when he met them by the river, camping. He kept this vision to himself. *Each must meet their fate,* he thought.

Soon after Sneener left the village, Goo Goo Ga Gus bought her a small home and land, and she still lives there, growing crops. People from the surrounding villages buy from her, and she's made a decent life for herself. She remains single, hoping one day she and Sneener will reunite. Once joining another tribe, they can't be together unless the kings of both tribes agreed to re-write the by-laws.

Who knows, she thinks. *Maybe enough time has passed that either King will let them be together.*

Her first memory of Sneener is a beautiful day after a rain, playing bones of the brach. This is a game when you stack bones of a brach (an animal resembling a pig) into a stack and whoever knocks the pile down first loses. Goo Goo Ga Gus beat Sneener in the game two out of three times.

He always claimed he let her win.

During the village festivals, Sneener and Goo Goo Ga Gus work as a team, beating out all the other groups. They are village champions four years in a row in hunting and field games.

By the time they are seventy, they realize they loved each other. Seventy in this land is young. Life destines them to be together. Goo Goo Ga Gus still loves Sneener, even though one hundred years separate them. Another fond memory she has is one time when they were thirty. They were babies. She snuck out of her parent's dwelling and ran down to the river to catch the sight of falling stars. If one sees twenty falling stars together in one sitting with their partner, they join in destiny forever. That night they see twenty-five. This makes Goo Goo Ga Gus the happiest girl in the village; the next day, she tells everyone, even her parents. She doesn't even get into trouble for sneaking out of their dwelling.

When Sneener leaves, she loses a piece of her heart that she knows she will never get back, and even worse when King RiRa banned him from the village, she lost the rest of her heart. Goo Goo Ga Gus isolates herself from friends and family and still prefers to be alone in her little dwelling on her small piece of earth. Goo Goo Ga Gus knows she will always love Sneener and that he loves her, and she has faith that he will come for her one day. When he does, she will leave with him.

Goo Goo Ga Gus spends her days and nights alone, working in her garden and selling her crops. At night, she sits by the fire reading ancient folklore, the folklore of humans visiting her soil. Humans from another world had been appearing in the land to accomplish essential tasks. She can recall hearing her great great parent talking of humans visiting. As a little girl, she remembers hearing stories of beings in her land that were part human. One story in particular was a being's father mated up with a female from the human world. She took the boy back to the human world and the father went into hiding. The story goes that she eventually brought the boy back to this world and she passed away here years later. Goo Goo Ga Ga Gus's great great parent said the boy's name was

Idaho Joe because his father visited from Idaho, a state in the human world.

Goo Goo Ga Gus prides herself on having free thoughts, and she realizes that nothing is impossible. Still, she has never completely bought into the whole other world or human thing. Some suggest the Gods choose humans to visit to satisfy a purpose. Other people say it is random, but either way, it is magic. Magic is ordinary in her land.

She understands why a human would want to come to her land because there is no violence.

Beings don't like each other sometimes, or they play tricks on each other, and some are not nice to others, but they do not understand violence, although she always wondered if Blue Bill is capable of understanding it. If there is another world, and humans visit this land, she hopes they take something back with them ending violence in their world.

"What are you doing right now, Sneener? Are you still in Ga Ga Galugas, or some other faraway village, do you think of me, my love?" she asks herself. On contemplation, she wonders if she made a mistake not going with Sneener.

"What does it matter?" she continues thinking. "I'm all alone anyway. If King RiRa would have banned me from Grangus, at least I would have been with Sneener."

Sadness doesn't exist in this land, but she sure is close to it if it did.

CHAPTER SIX

The next morning the rain stops, and the sun appears beautiful. Charlie and I get an early start. Two hours later, we reach the other side of the ridge to where Snakey says Blue Bill is camped. Snakey travels with us. When we arrive, the fire still smokes but no Blue Bill. The weather clears, so we ride further, hoping to find him.

Blue Bill sits looking into the crystal ball, and he can see us not far behind. Being low to the ground, Blue Bill moves slow.

We gain ground on him. Blue Bill hurries down the trail towards Grangus, planning to make Goo Goo Ga Gus his bride. Bill has not seen her in years and Sneener being back in the picture stirs old feelings in his heart.

We travel all day and stop in a clearing to rest. Once reaching the clearing, Charlie notices a river with a boat tied to a tree. As we come to the vessel, we meet a strange-looking fellow fishing.

"Hey O," the odd fellow says.

"Good day," I reply.

After explaining our journey, the strange fellow says he can guide us down the river in his boat.

"That will be helpful," I say.

We pile into the boat, and the weird-looking fellow paddles the boat down the river.

"Why do you have purple skin, mister," Charlie asks.

"Born that way."

Besides his purple skin, he has feet like a duck, his toes webbed together. This being's head is much smaller than the rest of his body and has long pink hair that stands straight up at least three feet upwards from his head.

Only thirty minutes downriver, we hit treacherous waters, scaring Charlie. Still, I hold on to him tight, reassuring him of our safety. I can feel his little body trembling. The water regains calmness as we float at a reasonable speed. I notice that the river turns and meanders in the opposite direction.

"Is this the right way?"

"Nope," the peculiar-looking fellow says. I have taken you four hours in the opposite direction away from Blue Bill. He can work magic through his crystal ball, remember? In other words, I am not real."

Then the strange-looking fellow vanishes. Luckily, the paddles don't. I paddle the boat to shore, realizing we will have to follow the river backward on foot by walking back to where we met the strange-looking fellow. It is too difficult to paddle that far upstream.

"The being is right, Charlie, Blue Bill can use magic in the crystal ball, he just tricked us."

"Bill is being sneaky to us, huh, Pah Pah."

"Yes, he is. I wish we still had that crystal ball."

"Me too Pah Pah."

THIS LAND IS SO BEAUTIFUL; I think as we walk, I can't help wonder why Charlie and I woke up in this place and why the blanket fort is magic. Also, how Charlie knew?

"Charlie, are you sure you want to continue? All we have to do is wish to go home."

"No, Pah Pah, we have to find Sneener."

Charlie and I arrive back to where we met the strange fellow. The two of us venture through a canyon where we stumble upon a floating cabin. This cabin hovers a foot from the ground and is the most exciting thing I ever saw.

"How does it do that, Pah Pah?

"Not sure, but it is kinda cool, huh?

"Yes."

We walk closer to the cabin where an elderly being stands on the edge of the porch leaning on a cane he made from a stick and says, "What in tarnation brings you two to these parts?"

"The boy and I are looking for a lost friend."

The old man asks us into his cabin where we sit for biscuits and pancakes. This ancient creature looks human, though short.

. . .

WE SIT as the old being stands at the fire, flipping cakes over up in the air. Every once in a while, he will check the biscuits over the fire, and as they are done, he limps over to the table, serving us with the pan of biscuits in one hand, the other grasping his cane.

"Are you human? Charlie asks.

"Partly," the old man answers.

His name is Idaho Joe, and he claims to be the nicest man on this side of Ga Ga Galugas. His mother from Idaho visited the land several hundred years ago, falling in love with Idaho Joe's father, who was native to the land.

"What did you do in our world, and how did you end up here?" I ask him.

Well, there is a story behind that. In your world, I was homeless."

"Homeless?" Charlie asks?

"Yep. Humans come here for a reason, to help most often. I have been here several hundred years, and I have found my reason. You fellers have to find yours."

"Tell us how you got here, Idaho," I ask.

"I still remember the day, still so fresh in my mind." Idaho Joe begins the story by saying, "See that sky, that's my roof. The ground is my floor, and the world is my domain."

Joe told Charlie and me that he was traveling on a train, and he said this phrase to a woman he was talking with.

"How far you going?" the woman asks.

"As far as this train will take me."

Life seems to guide Idaho Joe to Alabama to see his family. He appeared dirty and messy. Needed some washing up, but he doesn't smell too bad. He has a huge green backpack with a frying pan and a rolled-up tent tied to the bottom.

Joe tells Charlie and me how he shares his travels with this woman and how he winds up on the train departing Santa Fe. The lady listens to Joe's story, and the more he talks, the more fascinating she finds his tale.

The woman moves to the seat next to him as he tells his story. He sits with his arms crossed, looking at her now and then, making sure she is listening. The woman is wide-eyed, staring at him like she is frozen, enamored by his story. Even though she is sitting beside him, she is turned sideways in her seat, looking at him.

Idaho Joe tells his story with such passion that she stays onboard when her stop comes up. This woman turns out to be a writer offering to buy him supper if he tells her the rest of his story.

She rides the train to the end of the line where Joe de-boards. Joe speaks of his travels through Colorado and Northern New Mexico in the sixties. He came from Idaho when the hippies started communes in New Mexico and Colorado.

"Homelessness had its upside."

He talks about the sense of freedom that comes with it. No bills, no responsibilities to worry about.

"I had my tent and some clothes, and I panhandled a dollar or two for food, it wasn't all that bad."

The only real job he ever had was as a security guard

at a bank. He got fired for falling asleep. He's mostly picked up odd jobs, such as raking leaves, cutting grass, or unloading trucks.

"I began by telling this woman I was Joe and fifty-eight years old, raised in Mobile, Alabama. I mentioned I was thirteen when I left mobile in a traveling carnival passing through town on a cool October weekend."

"What about your parents?" Charlie asks. "Your parents just let you take off at age thirteen?"

"I was my parent, I suppose."

"Where are they now?"

"They passed many years ago. Anyway, back to my story, young Charlie."

The first destination with the carnival is Birmingham, hauling trash. Two ladies take a shine to him, protecting him as a little boy needs from the cruelties of the world. These women have their problems. They drink a lot and stay partying all night. Idaho said this set the pattern for his entire life.

Joe enjoys seeing happiness in children when they ride the carnival rides. Ruko, his boss, fired him for giving stuffed animals away to the children. Idaho Joe says he couldn't stand the heartbreak in their little eyes when they walk away from a game not winning. Joe stays under a bridge for a few days, where he meets up with another homeless person. They panhandle, making enough money for food. Together they travel around for a few weeks heading towards Florida, where the weather is warmer.

"Billy, the dude I traveled with, and I hit Orlando.

Billy got hit by a car as he wandered down the highway in the dark. Anyway, it kills him. Going through his pockets, I find an address in his jeans of a woman he has talked about finding in Orlando. So, what do I do? Well, I search for her."

Billy never talked much about this woman, other than he loved her and wanted to look her up.

"To make a long story short, I found and tell her I know Billy. This lady has money; it's obvious from her clothes and the Corvette she drives."

It turns out that this woman is Billy's sister. She buys me a meal and some new clothes, puts me up in a nice hotel for two nights, and gives me a hundred dollars.

"After a bath and a shave, I wander around Orlando for a couple of weeks and hitchhike towards California. Nothing pans out for me there, so I head for Lake Charles, Louisiana."

Joe eats from dumpsters, saying that sometimes restaurants throw fresh food in them.

"The clothes that Mary gave me were in good shape, so I guess I looked halfway presentable. One night, while walking down the street, a guy passes, turns around, and asks if I had an interest in making some money, so I went to work for this guy selling sewing machines. It didn't last long. I got fired for goofing off."

Idaho Joe bounces around panhandling, living on the streets for the next ten years. He ends up in West Texas, where he meets Rosa. Rosa is an alcoholic and not a nice person. Joe leaves town shortly after meeting her.

Joe says to the lady on the train, "This is when I

wander into Santa Fe. I've been here for the last several years. I made fifty dollars last week panhandling. That is how I can travel down to Mobile on this train. I talked to my brother, and he says that twisters destroyed his house. I figure I may as well do something productive with my time, so I'm headed down to help them clean up the mess."

The train rolls into the end of the line. Joe and the lady exit the train, and as promised, she buys him dinner.

Me, Charlie, and Idaho Joe are all sitting around the fire in his floating house as he shares this story with us. Charlie is doing everything he can to stay awake. I am sitting next to him as he lays his head on my shoulder. Idaho Joe stares straight ahead, lost in another world as he is telling us this story. The fire roars as if it is enjoying the story as well.

"The lady on the train asks me if I had the chance to live in a land where I could live to an ancient age and be happy, where time is different than in the human world would I go. I tell her yes. The woman says there is a place where it is possible. Fellows, I didn't believe her. Anyway, she also buys me a beer, which I drink in two gulps, and I fall asleep on the park bench. When I wake, I am here in this land. I meet the woman here again shortly after arriving, and she tells me my family history about how my mother visited this land and married a tribesman here, and they had me. All tribes of the land cast them away because he was a being, and my mother was human. My father stays in exile and my mother takes me back to your world. The state of Idaho. The woman on the train turns out to be my mother, and she came to bring me back here as it is safe for humans now. Well, I ain't totally human, but anyway she brings me back. That day on the train, she already knew who I was and found me on purpose, saying it was time for me to go home to the magic land, so here I am. Mary, my mother passed away several years ago. My purpose was to reunite with my mother and to come home."

CHAPTER SEVEN

"Now, gentlemen, tell me your stories. Why are you here and looking for Sneener?" Idaho Joe asks, so I tell him about Sneener and his banishment from Grangus. Idaho Joe is aware of the feud between him and Blue Bill and warned that Blue Bill is a magic expert.

"Yes, we know, he tricked us at the river," Charlie says.

"The strange-looking fellow image, yep, that's Blue Bill's favorite trick. How far it set you behind?"

"I'm not sure."

"Blue Bill performs well at that, but he is slow, and no magic can help him move any faster. First light I will help you fellers."

"You'll help us?" Charlie asks.

"I own a flying house, course I will help."

"Your house can fly?"

"Well, it's not floating here for nothing, young un', I tell you that."

That next evening the three of us sit in front of the fireplace, eating and talking. Idaho Joe shares folklore of his land, and Charlie and I tell stories of where we came from and the magic blanket fort, and how at this moment, we are sleeping back home in it.

Idaho is an excellent storyteller, and Charlie laughs and laughs at his stories. Joe tells of one story of bathing in the creek with his nah one hot summer day when a mess of snakes came swimming through the creek's muddy water.

"Snakey?"

"No not Snakey, young-un, I know Snakey, he is a nice snake. These are mean snakes; they are slopperchead snakes."

"Slopperchead snakes?"

"Yep, little one. Anyway, we were bathing in the creek, and Rover, my nah, sees the snakes swimming towards us, and so he barks the bark of the dead. I look across the

water's surface and see four of them swimming towards us, showing their fangs. They want us for lunch. Rover bites two in half, and I grab the other two by the tail, slinging them onto the bank where they crawl away."

"Wow! Idaho Joe."

"Wow is right, I was only six at the time."

The three of us drift off to sleep quickly. I on the floor with Charlie, using my arm as a pillow as Joe sleeps, sitting up in his rocking chair snoring like a freight train.

The next morning Charlie says he dreamed we found Sneener enjoying his days with Goo Goo Ga Gus.

Charlie cries when he realizes it is only a dream. Idaho Joe wakes early, making us breakfast, and after we clean up, we steer the house towards Grangus. We dodge the clouds, and Joe steers left and right, sharply shaking us around as we maneuver around them. Charlie thinks it so cool flying through the sky in a home. I have to agree; it is so cool. He looks down, viewing mountains, grass, and feeling the breeze in his face. The wind blows back my hair, and I feel at peace. Being in the air is quiet, almost like not being of any world, just free. Suddenly Charlie sees something on the ground shining so bright in the sun that it blinds him.

"Pah Pah, what's that shiny thing?"

"I don't know, but it is bright."

"Let's look," Idaho Joe says.

We touch down in a field of orange and brown plants. We jump out of the house and walk quickly through the overgrown plants finding this shiny object. To our surprise, it is Charlie's crystal ball. Blue Bill must have dropped it without realizing it. Now we have the magic, but other than using it as a guide, we still do not understand how to use it to perform magic. We need someone to show us how. This may also mean we were not too far behind Blue Bill. If one of us knew how to use the crystal ball, we could find him by looking into it.

"How about if we just ask it Pah Pah?"

"Maybe."

"Crystal ball, where is Blue Bill?"

Right before their eyes, the crystal ball reveals Blue Bill's location. He is only a mile ahead of us. With our floating house, we will catch him in plenty of time before he reaches Sneener.

"Is Sneener in Grangus?" Charlie asks the crystal ball.

The ball reveals Sneener in jail in the King's RiRa's castle.

"Is Goo Goo Ga Gus in Grangus?"

The crystal ball reveals she lives in a house outside the village.

"Charlie, you are the smartest little boy I ever saw," I tell him.

Blue Bill's aware the King is holding Sneener in the castle and aides protect Sneener from Blue Bill's harm, but Goo Goo Ga Gus is a sitting target for Blue Bill. We suspect her house on the outskirts of Grangus to be Bill's destination. That is where we will head for. Soon enough, we are up and away.

Just as Idaho Joe flies us over the mountain into a clearing, Charlie spots Blue Bill hiding behind a huge rock. That's the advantage of flying. In the sky, you can see almost everything below. Idaho Joe lands the house as close to Blue Bill's hiding place as he can get. We surround the rock but don't see Blue Bill. It is as if he vanished.

"Where did he go? Charlie asks.

"He will reappear, magic only lasts so long," says Idaho Joe.

"Only for so long?" Charlie asks.

"Yep."

"What now?"

"We go up again and see if we see him anywhere, and we continue to find Goo Goo Ga Gus."

"If Blue Bill has magic, why can't he just vanish and appear at Goo Goo Ga Gus's house?" Charlie asks.

"All who have powers have limitations. Maybe that's one of his, but we'll find him."

We fly for thirty minutes when a strong wind picks up. Idaho Joe lands the house because of these winds, which puts us a few hours behind schedule. Deciding to stop for the night, Charlie keeps asking to continue, but Idaho Joe feels like it isn't safe, as do I.

Relaxing in Idaho Joe's house, we find it comfortable and cozy. We all sit in the living room after dinner this evening as the wind whips and blows for hours. The fire is nice and warm, and our eyelids begin to get heavy. Our stomachs are full of rabbit meat and bread. We start talking about real and fiction stories as we sit around in a circle in front of the fire.

Not only is Joe a good storyteller, but I've also told a good story or two in my time. As we sit by the fireplace enjoying quosen, (tea of the land), Charlie says,

"Pah Pah, tell us a story."

"Sure, why not."

I settle back in my chair, clear my throat, and tell a story that Charlie had never heard before. It begins as a man and his son are walking across a crowded train platform. The snow is falling into a beautiful sight.

"Santa will be here soon," the man says to his son.

"Yes, and I have been a good boy this year."

"I know you have son."

They continue making their way across the crowded platform when the little boy glimpses a man ringing a bell asking for donations to help the animal rescue mission.

His father drops a five in the can, and the man ringing the bell looks up, smiles, and says, "Merry Christmas."

This isn't a regular five-dollar bill. This bill reads Merry Christmas and has the man's and a little boy's initials written on it in ink.

This man always writes friendly greetings or remarks on his bills. He doesn't have paper money often, so he blesses it with good energy when he does.

"Do you think the money will save an animal?" the little boy asks his dad.

"I hope so."

"Did it save an animal, Pah Pah?"

"Let me finish, grandbaby."

The little boy and his father continue walking down the sidewalk that runs along the street until they get to their home, which is a tarp stretched over some boxes. The man couldn't afford to have given five dollars to the man collecting for animals, but he did. The man and his son only have twenty dollars left to their name, and they still have to eat dinner.

———

Two MONTHS PASS, and somehow, the man and his son get through the harsh winter. Still, they struggle to find food every day, whether begging, sometimes even shoplifting, and any odd jobs the man can do to earn a dollar. Being on the street, he couldn't clean up to look presentable enough to find a job.

Meanwhile, at the shelter, a black lab is scheduled for euthanasia. The man asking for donations on that night searched the accounts for money to save this animal. Still, he was five dollars short of the daily minimum to hold an animal.

The man thinks he remembers sticking some money that night in the brim of his hat because his bucket began to overflow, and he didn't want to lose any bills. He knew his hat would be a safe place. He walks to the closet, pulls out the cap, and sure enough, five dollars is stuck in the brim that reads Merry Christmas and has the little boy's and father's initials written scribbled on it. These five dollars saved the dog. The next day a wealthy business owner adopts the dog, and the worker tells this man about the five-dollar bill and who it came from. The worker knew the man and his son. They had been homeless in that part of town for months. He tells the business owner where he can find the man and the boy.

The wealthy business owner finds the man and gives him money to clean himself up and gives him a job. After a while, the man saves money, buys a house, and now lives a happy life.

"That's the end, Charlie, it always pays to give when you can, rewards come back."

"It sure does, Pah Pah; that's a good story."

"Is that a true story?" asks Idaho Joe.

"It sure is."

Charlie's full of questions about the story.

Idaho Joe rises from his chair slowly as his bones creak, walking over to an old trunk stuck in the corner collecting dust. He opens it and tells Charlie there's something in it he wants him to have.

"A surprise?" asks Charlie.

"I suppose so."

Idaho Joe pulls out a worn brown leather pouch revealing a book. He opens it and gives it to Charlie. Since Charlie liked stories, Idaho Joe figures this book of stories will make Charlie happy and full of more questions.

"I can't read."

"You can read these stories because this book is magic."

"Magic."

"Yes, little one, yes, it is."

Sure enough, Charlie opens the book and reads a story of, believe it or not, a grandfather and his grandson who are the best of friends and who are out on an adventure.

"This is just like us, Pah Pah."

"It seems so."

"Why can't there be magic in our world?"

"There is magic in your world, it is just different magic."

The night grows old, and we retire for the evening in what I have to say is the most comfortable bed I have ever been in. Charlie snuggles up with me, asking even more questions about the story I shared, the stories he read in the magic book, and how he can even read them, as he doesn't know how to read yet.

I still question if all of this is real. Are Charlie and me still asleep in the tent dreaming these things, or are we really in a magic land? It seems real enough.

The next morning, we wake, have a good breakfast of some sort of eggs that I don't want to know what they are, and are off to find Blue Bill. We proceed in hopes of getting Sneener out of jail in Granges.

The house lifts off, and we are on our way, flying over the terrain to our destination. I enjoy seeing Charlie leaning against the porch railing, looking down below. The wind blows his hair back, and he has the most peaceful look I have ever seen. An hour passes, and below we see Blue Bill riding his animal across the green land. To our surprise, Blue Bill doesn't even try to hide. Idaho Joe lands the house a few yards in front of Blue Bill, and Blue Bill stops, gets down from his animal and sits on the ground.

"Bill, my son, it's been a long time," Idaho Joe replies.

"Yes, father, yes it has."

"Why don't you just let bygones be bygones? Goo Goo Ga Gus is living a happy life. Leave her be son. If you head back home, me and this man and his grandson can negotiate with King RiRa of Grangus for Sneener's release. You are complicating matters."

"I love Goo Goo Ga Gus and want to marry her. Haven't you ever been in love, father?"

"She loves Sneener, and once she finds out he's in the

village, if she hasn't already, she will head to Grangus and talk to King RiRa herself." Idaho Joe says.

"Sitting here, father I realize, I admire Sneener wanting to find his beloved Goo Goo Ga Gus. That is why I've decided to help them reunite. I don't feel well, I need rest."

"Come on in the house, I have a comfortable bed waiting for you."

Blue Bill falls asleep as we sit in the living room talking.

"You called him son," Charlie says to Idaho Joe.

"He is my son, Charlie, but I have not seen him in several years."

"I have not seen my Dad in years either, but Pah Pah teaches me."

"I am glad you have your Pah Pah."

"Me too."

"Blue Bill is really your son?" I ask.

"Yes, he is, sir."

Idaho Joe has not seen Blue Bill since he and Sneener were kids. Idaho Joe was so close with Blue Bill throughout his childhood and even into young adulthood. Blue Bill's mother passed, and things went bad between him and Goo Goo, so Blue Bill left home, losing contact with everyone.

"What happened to your wife?" asks Charlie.

"She drowned out in the river just down the way a piece."

"I'm sorry to hear that," I say.

"It was a long time ago."

Idaho describes how Blue Bill turned into a bitter person. Once he lost his mother, he became angry, seeking revenge for something that is nobody's fault. He just wants to blame someone for it. That someone is Sneener. Idaho Joe says Sneener was always a good being growing up and is a good man being. The night is long as Idaho Joe waits for Blue Bill to get his rest and wake up. He hasn't talked to his son for over sixty years. There is so much catching up to do. Idaho Joe still wants to help us with our journey. Now the focus is to talk with Sneener and find out what happened. Idaho Joe hopes his son's intention of assisting Sneener is real. Even though Blue Bill is his son, he will not allow him to hurt Sneener. They still have their work cut out for them. Sneener abandoned his tribe for the Ga Ga Galugas tribe, so it will not be easy persuading King RiRa to release him. This is all aside from whether Blue Bill will cause havoc on our journey. Plus, if he plans on doing so, Idaho Joe will have to ask Blue Bill to leave, risking never seeing him again. This is turning out a complicated journey.

Blue Bill wakes the next morning as his father sits by his bedside waiting.

"Father."

"Son, my dear son, I have missed you?"

"I too, father."

I see them hug and talk for hours, making amends to each other. Blue Bill apologizes for leaving his father, and Idaho Joe apologizes for letting him go without a fight. They also discuss their search for Sneener and Goo Goo Ga Gus.

"I love her father, I always have."

"Yes, son, but you have to let her go, she chose Sneener. We started on this trek to find Sneener, and why he has sought her now is not of my understanding, but he is in Grangus against his will. Your search and your interference for Goo Goo Ga Gus has distracted us, I ask that you work with us to persuade King RiRa to release him."

"I lost the crystal ball, without it I have no magic," Blue Bill says.

"Since when do you need it to work your magic?"

"I have not been the best instrument for magic. The God's took my magic from me right after I used the strange-looking fellow to take the boy and his Pah Pah off of my path."

"I'm sorry, son."

"I used it wrong. To get my magic back, I have to perform a good deed."

"Then help us. That will be the right deed."

"I will work with you, the Pah Pah, and Charlie to free Sneener. I will let Goo Goo Ga Gus go, as she loves Sneener. Not me.

Idaho Joe relays to Charlie and me that Blue Bill will help in the search but has lost his magic.

Charlie whispers in my ear, "He lost his magic Pah Pah, how will he help us?"

"The more manpower, the better."

"The more manpower the better," Charlie repeats.

"Always, grandson, always."

Blue Bill apologizes to us for what he has done, explaining that he lost his magic because of it.

The four of us continue with our journey to free Sneener. As we take off in the flying house, the steering system suddenly breaks, and we have to land. We land hard in the dirt. It shakes us to the bone. It gives Idaho Joe a chance to teach Charlie how to repair it. He loves teaching how to repair things. Charlie is a quick learner. He always had a knack for fixing or building something. After fixing the steering, we gather up our items and are off towards finding Sneener.

CHAPTER EIGHT

Meanwhile, on our way to Grangus, Sneener lay on his cot in his cell, looking up at the ceiling above, thinking about Goo Goo Ga Gus. Every once in a while, he will rise and pace back and forth, trying to figure out a way to get her a message that he is there. Then he will sit down and stare at the ceiling some more. He understands from asking questions to the King's men guarding him that Goo Ga Gus only makes her way to town three or four times a year. He pleads with the guards to get her his message, but they are too scared of King RiRa to carry this out. She has no way of knowing Sneener is in town. He has to get a message to her somehow. He also realizes that King Popo, by now, has sent out some beings to look for him as he has been gone four weeks. He knows this concerns King PoPo. Sneener figures beings had to have already been to Deeky's cabin looking for h
him.

Hum, I wonder how they are doing; it was nice meeting humans.

He also thinks of Blue Bill and wonders whatever happened to him. He knows that he isn't Blue Bill's favorite person but hopes they can patch things up someday if they ever crossed paths once again. Sneener has a lot of time to think while he's in his cell. His judgment is another week away, so he has plenty more time to contemplate. He has to figure out a way to get in touch with Goo Goo Ga Gus.

He isn't being treated so harshly, considering he abandoned his village so many years ago. It appears as though most people have either forgiven him, don't remember what he has done, or don't care, except for King RiRa. He will never forget. Sneener never liked how King RiRa treated the people in the kingdom. The King belittled the beings in front of others and their families. Sometimes he took things from them as a consequence for very minor offenses. RiRa picked and chose his favorites in town. He is about attaining riches for himself. Although his people don't do without, he could provide the inhabitants with much more. Sneener always had hopes that his family would prosper here instead of just getting by. His father and mother deserve more than what they have, but Sneener knows as

long as they are in Grangus, they will only get by.

Therefore, he left all those years ago. He wants more than to just get by; he wants to flourish. Moving to Ga Ga Galugas was the best decision, although he misses Goo

Goo Ga Gus. This is his only regret in the decisions he made.

He lies in his bed this evening as all evenings thinking about her. Thinking about what she is doing at that moment.

He remembers being with her at the river. They would lie down in the fields, looking up at the stars and moon, wishing they could fly up to where they were hanging so bright in the sky. He remembers one evening in particular when they lay there after a nice rain.

"What do you suppose is on the moon?" he asks Goo Ga Ga Gus.

"I don't know, perhaps other inhabitants, or some other life. Maybe that's where humans come from."

"Maybe so."

Will I ever see you again? Sneener asks himself on this evening sitting alone in his cell. He longs to talk and hold her hand, walking beside the river with her towards the sun. He has a recurring dream he knows is of her. This dream is of a female carrying flowers wearing a lavender wrap of some sort, maybe from the native trees of the magic land. In the dream, Sneener can't see her face. Every morning he wonders if it is Goo Goo Ga Gus, even though the roundness of her body doesn't look like her in his dream, but he feels it is.

In his dream, her right hand is on a basket's handle, her left holding the bottom. Her arms are positioned in a way as if she's about to hand him the flowers. Although blurry, behind her, Sneener can see the bush she picked them from. Her bristles full, but he's unable to tell if it is her natural texture or from the land's magic healing waters. She rolls closer to him, shrinking the distance between them as if to reach what she desires. He can only hope her desire is him. She's about to hand him flowers when he always wakes up.

Strange as it may seem, he falls in love with this being in his dream. Her bristles are beautiful. She looks sophisticated, warm, and friendly. Until now, he never realizes it is possible to love a faceless person of a dream. Everything he needs to know is in his image of her. Sneener loves her, and what her face looks like is not of concern. He doesn't care, he has fallen in love with

her, and she is beautiful. This is how he knows the faceless being in his dream is Goo Goo Ga Gus.

He risked a lot coming back to his village but hoped to see her at least for a little while before getting caught by the King's men. He thought about looking for her for years, and that day when he went to Deeky's checking on us, he can't explain, but that was the moment, so instead of going back home, he went off to find her. Never making it to her before being captured.

CHAPTER NINE

SIMULTANEOUSLY, AS SNEENER SITS IN HIS JAIL CELL, growing more impatient by the day, Goo Goo Ga Gus sits outside on her porch this summer evening. Feeling lost in thought, sipping a local tea, and humming an old folk song, she thinks of her past.

Since Sneener left years ago, she makes it a habit of staying out of town as much as possible. When she goes there, the memories flood her, and it is almost unbearable. Only venturing in when she needs to. Her life wasn't the same after Sneener left. Sometimes she thinks of him and regrets her decision of not going with him, and at other times she realizes she made the right decision.

She didn't know he would just up and leave, not that she thought he was bluffing, but she thought he would change his mind. He didn't though, he left.

Goo Goo Ga Gus will never forget the morning she realized Sneener gone. She was living in the town when she woke, poured her morning drink, and saw a note slid under her door.

My Dearest Goo Goo Ga Gus,

I regret not leaving with you, but I have to get away from here. I love you and always will, one day I will return for you, and together we will be forever.

Sneener

She falls to her knees, crying and cries for days.

In time hurt fades, and although she still thinks of Sneener and in some ways awaits his return, the sharpness of the hurt has long since dulled. It's because of her that Sneener and Blue Bill no longer hold their friendship.

This is a regret of hers even though it's their choice, it is over her. She expects to see Blue Bill cross her path before Sneener, but neither ever has.

Last she heard of Blue Bill, he was just wandering around aimlessly through the land picking up odd jobs from some of the lesser-known kings and villages. Goo Goo Ga Gus knows that Sneener lives in Ga Ga Galugas and tells herself that she will often visit, but she never does. She knows if she does, Sneener will talk her into staying with him, and she will, and as a result, she will be banned from her home. Goo Goo loves her household and doesn't want to put herself

in a position to be banned from it. So, she holds back from visiting him, although if sees him, she knows she will choose him this time.

Goo Goo Ga Gus missed Sneener for years, and sometimes she still finds his smells in particular flowers, foods, even sometimes in the air as she passes places they used to frequent. She dreams of Sneener and the times they had together. At first, waking in the morning from the dream seems so real. She wonders if Sneener's going through something. Perhaps this why she's dreaming of him so much as of late. She hopes not, wishing him well. She always feels sad that Sneener and Blue Bill's friendship ruined because of their love for her. It is sad to lose a good friend. Goo Goo Ga Gus also realizes she's been thinking of Sneener more often during her waking hours. Little does she know that Sneener is sitting in a cell in King Rira's court for the last two weeks. Goo Goo Ga Gus knows it's a long past time to let go. Some days it feels like she has. Other days it doesn't seem so. Goo Goo Ga Gus lives a good life, with position, family, and friends. She feels stable in her head and knows she is an ordinary being. She fell in love with him fast. Too fast, like in three months. They were going together for a hundred years when he left. They had not talked since the night before he took off. She has no hard feelings towards him. She wants him happy and hopes he finds, if not found, what he is looking for in existence, but sometimes she feels alone, and it makes her sad.

Thankfully, she has family, mother, father, sisters, brothers, and nah for conversation. Goo Goo's learned many things over the last two hundred years. The most important being the prize of family. Also, that she can be alone even though challenging.

She has learned that she doesn't need a relationship believing relationships are something one should wish, not need. However, she would be with Sneener in an instant.

She can't help but wonder if Sneener thinks of her or is having a hard time letting her go. She likes to believe so. Goo Goo Ga Gus tells her mother she doesn't understand why relationships are so hard. Mother tells her they are only as hard we make them. Her parents married over three hundred years ago. She hopes Sneener will come back and has faith he will when he is supposed to.

CHAPTER TEN

WHILE SNEENER AND GOO GOO GA GA GAUS ARE IN their thinking period. We travel all day, flying through thunderstorms, winds, and swarms of insects. We arrive in the village mid-afternoon and immediately go to the King's castle, asking to see Sneener. We walk through the streets up to the court and open the door to three guards sitting at a desk drinking root leaf mutton.

"We demand to see Sneener." little Charlie says.

The guard smirks and bounces up to Charlie as a tumbleweed in the wind back home in New Mexico. I think it startles Charlie at first.

"We know nothing of a Sneener."

Charlie shows the guard the crystal ball and tells him they see Sneener locked up somewhere in this castle. The guards look at each other.

"Very well then," and they lead us to an underground cell. The cells are a dirt-walled room with small tree limbs as bars. When Sneener sees Blue Bill, he is skeptical as he backs up from the bars cautiously. Idaho Joe assures him that Blue Bill reformed his ways and wants to reunite him and his beloved Goo Goo Ga Gas. Sneener is glad to see Charlie and me, however. Sneener explains everything.

When Sneener leaves Deeky's cabin after checking on us, a sudden angst, an intense un-fightable desire comes over him. He admires the bond Charlie and I have together. Inspired by our adventure to his land, it motivates him. He takes a risk, just as we have, not by exploring new lands as us, but by deciding to ride to Grangus to find Goo Goo Ga Gus. He knows if found snooping around the village, King RiRa will put him in jail. That's ok because he wants to find his lost love. He has not seen her in a long time.

Even as he sits locked in his cell, he thanks Charlie and me for inspiration to find his beloved Goo Goo Ga Gus.

"Does she know you are here?" Charlie asks.

"No. If she did, she would talk to the King for my release."

"We will bring her."

So, with those words, we are off to Goo Goo Ga Gus's house to tell her Sneener is a prisoner in King RiRa's castle. Charlie can't wait to tell her that Sneener has come to reclaim his love for her. We arrive after crossing the windy prairie and finding Goo Goo Ga Gus on her front porch gazing up into the sky. We introduce ourselves and tell her our mission. She falls over unconscious for a few seconds as she feels overwhelmed that

Sneener is in town. Within an hour, we cross the windy prairie heading into Grangus and are all standing before Sneener. He and Goo Goo Ga Gus reunite after many years. They are separated by the stick bars, but they can still hold hands, and this is the most peace either of them has felt in over a hundred years.

"I love you so much, Goo Goo Ga Gus, I came for you, to take you back with me."

"I love you too, Sneener, I am sorry I didn't go with you, I will now, I am ready."

Turns out Goo Goo Ga Gus is King RiRa's sister, so she has easy access to him.

"Guards, I want to see my brother now!"

She proposes to the King for Sneener's release under the condition Sneener will exit the village never to return. Goo Goo Ga Gus also tells her brother he owes her this for putting her through years of torture, by banning her love from the village.

"If you don't release Sneener, I will leave and take the family with me, never to return, and you will be alone for the rest of your life."

"Your threats don't scare me, sister. I am old. Who knows how long I will live anyway?"

"Also, brother, I am leaving with Sneener and I want to be able to return and not be banished. Sneener agrees to comply with his banishment, but I will not be banished."

"Those demands are preposterous, sister. No"

At that moment, Snakey slithers from deep within Charlie's pack, poking his head out and flinging himself to the floor. He slithers to where King RiRa stands and slithers up his leg, his arm, and to his face. King RiRa freezes like a statue. He is terrified, he cannot move. His breath is short and his bristles turn dark brown.

King RiRa stares straight ahead, not moving any part of his body except for his

mouth.

"Snakey!! I thought you were dead."

"Well, I ain't."

"I am working with my friends and you will abide by their wishes."

Snakey is one of the last snakes in the land that can cast spells on Kings for their indiscretions. Most of them were captured during the King Snake wars of two hundred years ago and sent to the other world as regular snakes, but Snakey remains.

"King RiRa if you don't let Sneener go, you indeed will be alone as Goo Goo Ga Gus will take the family away. I will curse you to live forever, and forever you will be without your family. That is a long time to be alone. I will take everyone from you. Your guards, your associates, your nahs. You will utterly be alone."

King Ri Ra frees Sneener as he is terrified by Sankey's threat.

His beloved Goo Goo Ga Gus vows Sneener's love and leaves with us, returning to King PoPo's kingdom. After a two-day journey, Charlie, Idaho Joe, Blue Bill, Sneener, Goo Goo Ga Gus, Snakey, and I are back in Ga Ga Galugas before King PoPo. We share our adventure with the King. The King mentions that everything in life happens for a reason. He continues to say that Charlie and I venturing to this land is twofold. One, so that Sneener could reunite with Goo Goo Ga Gus. Two, if not for a grandfather and grandson's love for adventure, Sneener would not have felt inspired to take a risk to find her. The other reason is that their desire to help a friend in need served as an avenue for Idaho Joe and his son Blue Bill to reunite. If Charlie and I hadn't been on this search, they would not have crossed paths with Blue Bill, leading him to Idaho Joe. After an enormous feast, King PoPo urges us to stay, but Charlie misses his mom, so we decide to return home.

We woke the next morning back in the magic tent fort.

"Pah Pah, wake up."

"I'm awake."

Charlie tells me of his dream, and I say I had the same one.

"Was it real, Pah Pah?"

"No, grandbaby, it wasn't real."

Charlie feels something at his feet. He pulls back the covers, and there lies the crystal ball they used as their guide to find Sneener.

"It was real, Pah Pah. It was real."

The End

Dear reader,

We hope you enjoyed reading *The Magic Blanket Fort*. Please take a moment to leave a review, even if it's a short one. Your opinion is important to us.

Discover more books by Keith Kelly at https://www.nextchapter.pub/authors/keith-kelly

Want to know when one of our books is free or discounted? Join the newsletter at http://eepurl.com/bqqB3H

Best regards,
Keith Kelly and the Next Chapter Team